the Wise Fool

Retold by DENYS JOHNSON-DAVIES

Sewing by HANY EL SAED AHMED
from drawings by HAG HAMDY
MOHAMED FATTOUH

PHILOMEL BOOKS

FOR LISA AND LUKE   —DJD

TO MY FATHER HAG FATTOUH   —HF

With special thanks to Sarah Gauch, who discovered Hag Hamdy and Hany in Cairo
and assisted the editors in working across an ocean.

PATRICIA LEE GAUCH, EDITOR

Design by Semadar Megged.
Text set in 16-point Mrs Eaves Roman.
The artwork was created with hand-sewn tapestries, known as *khiyamiyas* in Egypt.

PHILOMEL BOOKS
A division of Penguin Young Readers Group
Published by The Penguin Group
Penguin Group (USA) Inc., 375 Hudson Street, New York, NY 10014, U.S.A.
Penguin Group (Canada), 10 Alcorn Avenue, Toronto, Ontario, Canada M4V 3B2 (a division of Pearson Penguin Canada Inc.)
Penguin Books Ltd, 80 Strand, London WC2R 0RL, England.
Penguin Ireland, 25 St. Stephen's Green, Dublin 2, Ireland (a division of Penguin Books Ltd.)
Penguin Group (Australia), 250 Camberwell Road, Camberwell, Victoria 3124, Australia (a division of Pearson Australia Group Pty Ltd).
Penguin Books India Pvt Ltd, 11 Community Centre, Panchsheel Park, New Delhi - 110 017, India.
Penguin Group (NZ), Cnr Airborne and Rosedale Roads, Albany, Auckland 1310, New Zealand (a division of Pearson New Zealand Ltd).
Penguin Books (South Africa) (Pty) Ltd, 24 Sturdee Avenue, Rosebank, Johannesburg 2196, South Africa.
Penguin Books Ltd, Registered Offices: 80 Strand, London WC2R 0RL, England.

Library of Congress Cataloging-in-Publication Data
Johnson-Davies, Denys.
The adventures of Goha, the Wise Fool / retold by Denys Johnson-Davies ; sewing by Hany El Saed Ahmed
from drawings by Hag Hamdy Mohamed Fattouh.   p. cm.
Summary: A collection of fifteen tales about the folk hero Nasreddin Hoca, also known as Goha, a man with a
reputation for being able to answer difficult questions in a clever way.   1. Nasreddin Hoca (Legendary character)
2. Tales—Turkey. [1. Nasreddin Hoca (Legendary character) 2. Folklore—Turkey.] I. Ahmed, Hany El Saed, ill.
II. Fattouh, Hamdy Mohamed, ill. III. Nasreddin Hoca (Anecdotes). English. IV. Title.   PZ8.1.J639Go 2005
398.2'09561'02—dc22   2004015739
ISBN 0-399-24222-8
10 9 8 7 6 5 4 3 2 1
First Impression

Contents

Goha Carries the Basket

s usual, once or twice a week, Goha put a saddle on his donkey and rode off to the market to buy the freshest fruits and vegetables that were in season. This time, with the full basket slung over his shoulder, Goha got back on the donkey.

On his way home, his friend stopped him and asked, "Wouldn't it be easier to put the basket in front of you on the donkey? After all, isn't that why you took the donkey to the market?"

"But that wouldn't be fair to my good donkey," Goha answered. "Isn't it enough that the poor animal is carrying me? The least I can do is to carry the basket."

Goha and the Shoes

ome friends of Goha decided to play a trick on him. They knocked on his door, pretending that he had invited them to his house for lunch that day. Goha was embarrassed. He was by nature a good and generous man, but—he did not remember inviting them for lunch.

But he said, "Welcome, friends. Welcome," and, after they had left their shoes at the door, which was their way, he showed them into the parlor.

Then, quickly, he rushed off to his wife and told her what happened. "But, Goha," she said, "there's no food in the house! How could you invite them for lunch?"

"I didn't invite them!" Goha said.

"Ah," said his wife, "they're trying to trick you. Leave them in the parlor; they'll get tired of waiting soon enough and they'll go home."

Goha left them in the parlor laughing at the trick they had played on him and waiting for their meal. But Goha decided to play his own trick. He sneaked to the door, collected all the shoes they had left by the door, and hurried off to the market, where he sold the shoes!

Then he took all of the money he received for selling them and quickly bought some food for the meal.

Finally, his wife prepared the meal. Everyone ate well, for they had waited so long, they were hungry. But when they came to say good-bye to Goha, none of them could find their shoes.

"Where are our shoes?" they barked at Goha.

"Your shoes," Goha answered calmly, "are now in your stomachs!"

Goha Counts His Donkeys

oha noticed that the merchant life was a good life. He decided he would become a merchant, and buy and sell donkeys.

Happily, he went off to the marketplace, where he looked over many donkeys. Finally, he bought twelve of the best. Now, he thought, I will take them home. Tomorrow I will become a merchant.

So, he climbed onto one of the donkeys, and prodding the others in front of him, he thought, I might as well count my donkeys. So, he counted. One, two, three, four, five six, seven, eight, nine, ten, eleven . . . Eleven donkeys!

But he had just bought twelve donkeys. Shaking his head, he climbed down from his donkey and counted again. One, two, three, four, five, six, seven, eight, nine, ten, eleven . . . twelve! Now there were twelve. That was better.

Happy again, he climbed back onto the donkey that he had been riding. Just to make certain, though, he counted his donkeys again. There were only eleven! Again, he climbed down and counted—there were twelve.

He scratched his head. Sometimes there were eleven and sometimes there were twelve. "But," he said, "if I walk, I gain a donkey, which is better than riding and losing a donkey."

So he walked all the way to his house behind the twelve donkeys that he had bought at the market.

Goha Goes to a Party

t was a beautiful afternoon and Goha was out enjoying a gentle walk around the town. Suddenly a stone landed right by him. He turned around and saw that some boys were throwing stones at him.

"Shall I throw stones back, or shall I run away?" he asked himself. Then he had a good idea, and he called out to the boys:

"Hey! If you stop throwing stones, I'll tell you some good news!"

The boys stopped throwing stones. "Tell us. Tell us!" the boys shouted.

"The governor is holding a party at his palace. There are tables full of cream cakes, and everyone's invited!"

In a flash the boys raced off down the road to the palace, while Goha stood and watched them. Then, suddenly, he too started running toward the palace.

"After all," he told himself as he ran, "it just might be true!"

Goha Wonders Where the Cat Is

oha suddenly felt like having a really good meal that evening, so he went to the market and bought three pounds of the best lamb, which he took back home.

"Here," he said to his wife, giving her the three pounds of lamb. "Cook this. It will make a splendid meal."

Goha's wife, who was an excellent cook, cut the meat into pieces and prepared various vegetables and, of course, some rice, which she put into the steaming pot. Finally, she put the meat into the stew to cook. Soon the whole house was filled with the delicious smell of lamb stew bubbling away.

Now it so happened that the wife of Goha's neighbor had some visitors, and they smelled the delicious stew. "Let's visit her," one said. So they went off next door, where they all bent around the cooking pot.

"Let's just try a tiny piece," said Goha's wife, putting a spoon into the steaming stew and eating a piece of meat. Then each of the women put a spoon into the pot, and ate a piece of meat. "Very tasty. Very tasty," they said.

Again they sampled the stew. Again and again. And so it went all afternoon. Soon all the meat was gone. With horror Goha's wife looked into the pot. Her husband's supper had disappeared!

When Goha arrived home, his wife met him and told him that all she had for his supper were some vegetables and a pot of rice.

"What about the three pounds of meat that I bought?" Goha asked.

"Dear husband, that wicked cat of ours sneaked into our kitchen and stole it all when my back was turned."

Goha went off in search of the cat, carried it into the house, and put the cat on a pair of scales. Its weight was exactly three pounds!

"If this is the cat, dear wife, then where's the meat? But if this is the meat, then where's the cat?"

Goha Goes for a Swim

t was such a boiling hot day that Goha could think of nothing more pleasant than taking a dip in the river. He therefore undressed and left his clothes in a neat bundle on the riverbank.

But when he came out from his dip in the cool water, Goha found that someone had made off with his clothes.

So, having learned his lesson, the next time he went for a swim in the river, He went in fully clothed. When people saw him coming out of the river with soaking wet clothes, they laughed at him.

"How stupid of you!" they told him. "Whoever goes for a swim wearing all of his clothes?"

"Only someone," Goha answered, "who prefers to be wearing his clothes wet than have someone else wearing them dry."

Goha Goes Hunting Bears

ne day, the governor of the town invited Goha to go on a bear hunt with him. He liked Goha's amusing conversation. Now, the truth is Goha wasn't very keen on hunting bears—the idea made him shake. But when somebody as important as the governor invites you to do something, you'd better accept.

So Goha spent a day climbing about in the mountains, hunting bears.

On getting back to town, Goha was asked by his friends whether the bear hunt had been successful.

"Completely successful," said Goha.

"How many bears did you chase in the mountains?" one friend asked.

"None," said Goha.

"How many bears did you kill?" a friend enquired.

"None," said Goha.

"How many bears did you see?"

"None," said Goha yet again.

"But how, then, can you say that it was a successful bear hunt when you didn't even see a single bear?"

Goha nodded his head as he replied, "Friends, when hunting bears, it's best if you don't see a single one."

Goha Tricks the Robbers

oha was walking along a road near his hometown when two men jumped out from the bushes, threatening him with knives.

"Either you hand over your money or we'll kill you," said one of the men, pointing his knife at Goha's throat.

As it happened, Goha had no money with him. He was about to tell them that he didn't have any money, but realized that this might enrage his attackers and make them cut his throat.

"You know," Goha said to the two robbers, "today is your lucky day, because I am by chance carrying a large amount of money with me."

The faces of the two robbers lit up with joy at Goha's words.

"Then hand the money over and we'll let you go," they told him.

"Oh no," said Goha. "I think that I should give the money to just one of you. Why don't you agree between you who should have the money."

Immediately the two robbers began shouting and arguing. All too soon the argument turned into a fight with fists, kicks and then with knives! For a time, Goha stood and watched them. Then, seeing they were more interested in their fight than in him, he slipped away and continued his walk.

Goha and the Twenty Geese

ne of Goha's neighbors came to him. It was still morning.

"Goha, my friend," he said, "would you be so good as to look after my geese for a few days while I am away on business?"

"With pleasure," Goha answered. "Just drive the geese into my yard where I can give them water and food."

The next day the man brought along his honking geese. "There are twenty of them in all," he told Goha.

"I'll keep an eye on them," Goha told him.

But when the neighbor returned to Goha's house several days later, he counted his geese and discovered there were only nineteen!

"One of my geese is missing," said the neighbor. "Goha, my friend, perhaps you had one for dinner."

"If I'd done that, I would have told you," Goha answered him.

"Perhaps then a fox got in one night and made off with a goose," the neighbor suggested.

"Certainly no fox got into my yard," said Goha. "When you drove your geese into my yard, you said there were twenty. Well, my friend, then there are twenty still."

The two men continued to argue, with the neighbor counting nineteen and Goha insisting that there were twenty geese.

The neighbor was growing very angry, certain that Goha had stolen a goose. Finally, he said, "Let's go to the judge, then. Let us see which of us is right."

When the judge heard the problem, he scratched his beard. He knew the neighbor would not lie, and he knew Goha would not steal a goose. So, he ordered twenty policemen to be brought into the courtroom at the same time the geese were driven in.

"There are twenty policemen in front of you, true?" he asked Goha.

"That's true," Goha said. "There are twenty policemen in front of me."

"Now if each policeman takes hold of one goose, there will be twenty geese," said the judge.

"Yes," said Goha. "That is true."

Each of the policemen picked up one goose. But when they were done, one of the policemen was standing empty-handed.

The judge said to Goha, "Goha, you can now see that one of the twenty policemen does not have a goose. What's the reason for that?"

"The reason is simple, Your Honor," Goha answered immediately. "That policeman without a goose is a fool. The geese were all there in front of him—what was he waiting for? Why didn't he do as the others did and pick up a goose?"

Goha Refuses to Say a Word

oha's wife did all the housework and cooking, washing their clothes and a hundred and one jobs around the house. Goha was responsible for the donkey. It was Goha's job to go out into the yard and feed the donkey twice a day.

Today, though, Goha felt plain tired and lazy. "You feed the donkey," he said to his wife. "Just for today."

"No," said Goha's wife. "It's your donkey, and it's you who are responsible for going out and feeding it."

This started a big argument, with Goha saying, "It isn't asking too much of you to feed the donkey just this once," and Goha's wife saying, "No! I have my own work to do. It's your donkey!"

Finally Goha said, "I have an idea. The first one of us to speak feeds the donkey. Agreed?"

"Agreed," said Goha's wife.

So Goha went and sat in a corner of the room, determined not to speak, while his wife did what she always did around the house. But it was so quiet!

Feeling that she couldn't bear being in a house that was so quiet, Goha's wife decided to dress up and go for a walk.

When she returned home, she found Goha still seated in his corner, not speaking. So she went out again, this time to pay a visit to her neighbor.

"Welcome, my dear," said the neighbor.

The only reply Goha's wife made was to point to her throat.

"You poor thing, you have a sore throat. I'll make you some hot lemon and sugar."

Goha's wife thanked the woman with a smile.

It was only when she had drunk the hot lemon that she realized that Goha was alone in the house and hadn't had any supper! With movements of her hand and mouth, she made her neighbor understand that her husband needed something to eat.

"Ah, I understand," the kind neighbor said. "I'll have my son go around to your house with a bowl of soup for him."

During this time a thief had entered Goha's house and had taken away everything of any value—pillows, hangings, a tea set and more. He had noticed a man sitting in a corner who said not a word, even when his house was being burgled. Before he left, the burglar went up to Goha and took away his large turban.

Still Goha did not utter a word!

So the burglar tucked the turban in the sack with everything else, and sneaked away from the house.

He had just left when the neighbor's son brought the soup and found Goha still sitting silently like a statue.

"Good evening, Sheikh Goha," said the boy, but Goha made no reply to his greeting.

"My mother has sent this warm bowl of soup for you," said the boy.

Goha said nothing. Instead he made sweeping gestures to show that the house had been burgled and pointed to his head to show that even his turban had been stolen.

The boy, who was not too bright, thought Goha wanted the soup to be poured over his head. The hot soup flowed down Goha's face.

Goha scowled furiously at the boy, but still he did not speak.

When Goha's wife returned and found the house upside down, her pillows, hangings and tea set gone, and her husband sitting there with a bare head and soup all over him, she screamed, "What is going on here?"

At these words, Goha's face broke into a triumphant smile. "I won!" he shouted out. "Now you go and feed the donkey!"

The Thieves Visit Goha

n the middle of one night, Goha heard sounds in the house and realized that a thief was wandering around, searching for something to steal.

Goha climbed out of bed very quietly and hid in a cupboard.

The thief moved around the rooms. Finally, finding nothing to steal, he came to the big cupboard. Smiling, he opened the cupboard door—and saw Goha.

The thief was surprised! "What are you doing here in the cupboard?" he said to Goha.

"Pardon, dear sir, pardon," Goha said, "I felt so bad to know that you would find nothing in my humble house to steal, that I hid myself in here out of embarrassment."

Goha Has the Last Word

Goha decided that he would like to go to the public baths! He had never been before. So, dressed in his rumpled, everyday pants and shirt, he went, but the bath attendants looked down at him. They handed him a tiny piece of soap and a small, dingy bath towel.

Goha liked the steamy baths, but while sitting around after having his bath, he noticed other customers, wrapped in big, fluffy towels, served glasses of tea and plates of cakes full of honey and nuts. But not him!

Goha was not happy at the way he had been treated, but on leaving, he tipped each of the attendants with a gold coin.

"Thank you very much, sir," they said, bowing down low. This man in his poor, rumpled clothing was so generous! They whispered to themselves that if he came to the baths again, they would give him their very best attention.

The following week, Goha again put on his rumpled, everyday clothes and made another visit to the public baths. The attendants saw him coming, and remembered how generous he had been. They treated him like a king. They gave him a perfumed soap and a beautiful, white, fluffy towel. After the bath, they served him a steaming glass of tea and a plateful of delicious cakes.

This time, on leaving the baths, Goha gave each of the attendants the smallest copper coin he could find.

The men's faces fell. They were surprised and disappointed too.

"You see," said Goha, "the copper coins I have just given you are for the first visit I made to the baths, when you treated me like a beggar. The gold coins I gave you on that first visit were for the extra service I had today.

"Be careful not to judge people by appearance," Goha said, and he left the baths, whistling.

Goha Gives His Son a Lesson About Life

oha was a man who didn't worry about what other people might think about him. "Do what you believe is right," he would say, "and let people think what they like."

But Goha had a son who was always worrying about what people would say or think about him. Goha wanted to teach him a lesson.

So Goha saddled his donkey and asked his son to accompany him to the next village. With Goha riding the donkey and his son walking behind them, they passed by some men gathering at a coffee shop.

"Look at that selfish man who rides the donkey and makes his poor son walk," one man whispered to another.

So Goha got down from the donkey and told his son to get on. Goha would walk.

Now they passed by another gathering of people at a marketplace, who pointed at the boy. "Just look at the boy, letting his poor father walk. He has no manners and no respect for grown-ups."

So Goha climbed up behind his son, and they both rode the donkey.

"Poor donkey," some people standing near the road said, "and how unfair that he has to carry the man and the boy."

So Goha and his son carried the donkey between them. "Now, let's see what people have to say," Goha said.

Of course, now everyone laughed at them. "How ridiculous of that madman and his son, trying to carry the donkey instead of riding it!"

When the donkey was once again walking on its own four legs, Goha turned to his son and said, "You should know, my son, that in life, it is impossible to please everyone. So do not spend time worrying about what people think."

Goha Decides to Buy a New Donkey

othing was more important to Goha than his donkey. It was not only his way of getting around the town and of visiting his friends, which he liked to do, but he was also really fond of his donkey, which he had had for many years.

But one day a friend suggested to Goha that he should get himself a new donkey, one that was younger, more comfortable to ride and perhaps able to run faster than his present donkey.

Goha scratched his head and said to himself, "Maybe he's right. It is time to get a new donkey."

Before getting himself a new donkey, though, Goha had to sell his present one. So, he took his donkey to the market and handed it over to the man who bought and sold donkeys, mules and horses.

Immediately the turbaned man announced in a loud voice: "Donkey for sale!" and a large crowd collected.

The man stepped around the donkey, showing it to the gathering crowd, then began describing it:

"Look what a fine donkey I have here. The best!" he shouted as he stroked the donkey's ears. "See how quiet and gentle it is! Look at its powerful muscles!" More and more people circled the donkey. "Why, this animal is more like a racehorse than a donkey!"

Having listened to all this praise of his donkey, Goha couldn't help telling himself: "Good heavens, that's just the sort of donkey I'm looking for!" And he stepped up to buy his own donkey.

Goha Outthinks the Three Wise Men

Three wise men from a faraway country came to the town in which Goha lived. During the dinner the governor gave for them at the palace, the three men asked if in the town there were wise men to whom they could put certain difficult questions.

The governor scratched his head, then thought of Goha, who had the reputation for being able to answer difficult questions in a clever way. "Bring Goha to the palace," he ordered one of his men.

So Goha dressed up in his best clothes and wound around his head the biggest possible turban so as to make himself look like a wise man.

In the courtyard of the palace Goha found that all the town's leading citizens had come to see how he was going to answer the questions of the three wise men.

No sooner had he dismounted from his donkey than the first wise man came up to Goha and said: "Tell us, O wise Sheikh, where is the middle of the earth?"

Without a second's hesitation, Goha pointed with his stick to the spot where the donkey had placed its left front foot. "Just under there," said Goha, "is the exact middle of the world."

"What proof do you have of that?" demanded the first wise man.

"If you refuse to take my word for it," answered Goha, "then dig down and see for yourself. If you find that I am wrong, then you have every right to call me an ignorant fool."

The three wise men exchanged looks and kept silent.

Then the second wise man asked, "How many stars are there in the sky?"

Without any hesitation, Goha answered: "The very same number as the hairs on my donkey."

"And how do you know that?" demanded the second wise man.

"If you don't believe me, then count the hairs on my donkey," said Goha.

"And how can anyone possibly count the hairs on a donkey?" the second wise man asked angrily.

"And the stars in the sky?" Goha answered him. "Can they be counted?"

The three wise men just looked at one another. They had no answer for that.

Then the third wise man asked, "All right, if you have an answer for everything, how many hairs are there on my head?"

Right away, Goha replied, "The very same number as the hairs on my donkey's tail."

"And how can you prove that?" asked the third wise man, certain that he had stumped Goha.

"Pull one hair from your head, and then one hair from my donkey's tail. If in the end you have the same number of hairs from your head as from my donkey's tail, then I am right. If you do not, then I am wrong."

The three wise men burst into laughter.

"Bravo!" they said. "Sheikh Goha, you have shown yourself to be a man of great wisdom. How were you able to give us such clever replies to questions to which most people have no answers?"

Goha said to them: "If you are faced with a question to which there is no sensible answer, then any answer will do!"

IN CAIRO'S OLD ISLAMIC QUARTER, just beyond a huge medieval gate called Bab Zuwayla, lies the Street of the Tentmakers, or *Sharia Al Khiyamiya* in Arabic. Built 350 years ago of sturdy rose and beige stone, it is one of Cairo's last covered markets. And although the timber roofing casts shadows across this closed, narrow road, there is enough noise, color and commotion inside to brighten the whole street. Men of all ages sit cross-legged on platforms inside the one-room stores, meticulously sewing wall hangings, pillows, bedspreads and table covers, a kaleidoscope of colors in Islamic and pharaonic patterns that cover the walls of their shops.

In one of these small, stone stalls, the one with the sign above reading Fattouh Sons, sit Hag Hamdy and Hany, the illustrators of this book of Goha stories. Like

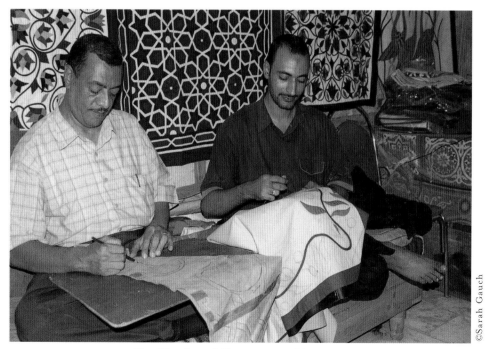

Hag Hamdy and Hany creating khiyamiyas

all the others, they, too, sit cross-legged, quietly drawing or hand sewing their colorful designs.

Centuries ago, when the tentmakers first began their work, they mainly made huge tents that were used for weddings, funerals and religious holidays in detailed geometric designs that resembled the wall and floor patterns of Cairo's medieval mosques.

Today they also sew village scenes of local folk, like Goha. It seems that every tentmaker has a Goha—paunchy Gohas and skinny Gohas, Gohas with beards and Gohas without, turbaned Gohas, smiling Gohas and bug-eyed Gohas. But whatever the Goha, it seems the favorite story is the tale "Goha Gives His Son a Lesson About Life," where Goha and his son listen too much to what others say and end up carrying their donkey instead of riding him.

It's unknown where exactly Goha came from—several Middle Eastern countries claim he originated with them. Some say he is make-believe, while others say he was a real man, a self-proclaimed preacher, who was born in a small Turkish village in the thirteenth century. Even Goha's name is disputed. In Egypt he is Goha, but in some other Arab countries he is Juha. In Turkey he is Hoja Nasrudin, and in Iran, Mulla Nasrudin. Whatever his name and origins, Goha's character is always the same—sometimes foolish, sometimes wise, and at other times a trickster who makes others the fool. Set in medieval teahouses, bathhouses and marketplaces, Goha's stories have been passed down for centuries, spreading across the Middle East and to neighboring Muslim countries. In fact, his stories are so funny, insightful and clever that they can be enjoyed across continents, by generations and in many languages.

SARAH GAUCH
Cairo, Egypt